P. 4 Here Comes Diego!   P. 5 Animal Rescuer!   P. 6 Feathered Friends   P. 7 Baby Jaguar

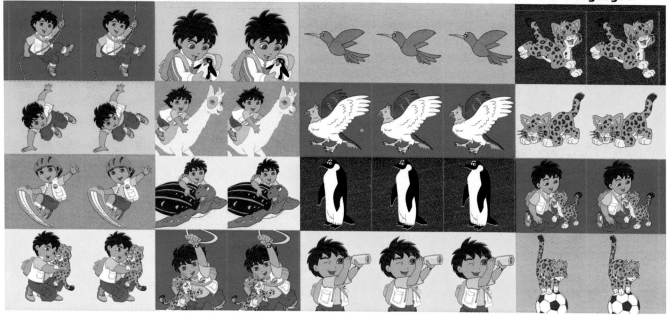

P. 8 Water Action!   P. 9 African Adventure!   P. 10 Goooaaalll!

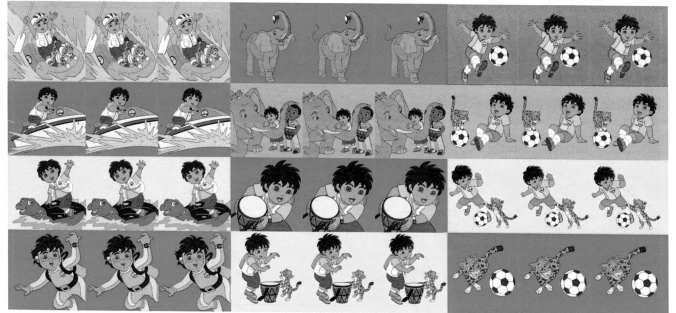

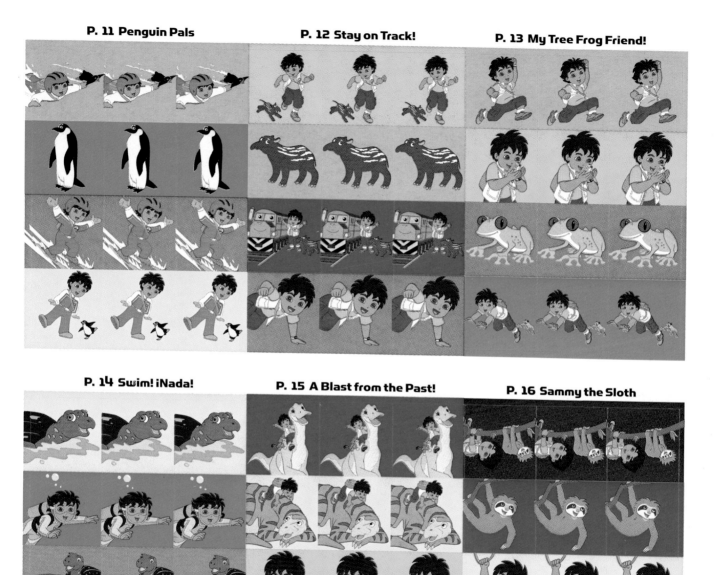

P. 11 Penguin Pals

P. 12 Stay on Track!

P. 13 My Tree Frog Friend!

P. 14 Swim! ¡Nada!

P. 15 A Blast from the Past!

P. 16 Sammy the Sloth

By YOE! Studio®

Based on the TV series *Go, Diego, Go!*™ as seen on Nick Jr.®

SIMON SPOTLIGHT/NICK JR.
An imprint of Simon & Schuster Children's Publishing Division
New York London Toronto Sydney
1230 Avenue of the Americas, New York, NY 10020
© 2007 Viacom International Inc. All rights reserved.
NICK JR., *Go, Diego, Go!,* and all related titles, logos, and characters are
trademarks of Viacom International Inc.
Manufactured in the United States of America
First Edition
2 4 6 8 10 9 7 5 3 1
ISBN-13: 978-1-4169-3555-1
ISBN-10: 1-4169-3555-X

You don't need to be a rainforest explorer to solve sudoku puzzles—you just need your brain and some logic!

There are more than 200 stickers included in this book!

Use the stickers from each set to complete each puzzle. Each sticker goes in a blank square in the puzzle. There are also some extras to stick anywhere you like!

Here's the only rule:

Each picture can appear only once in each row, column, and box of squares!

Get ready to race into action and solve some sudoku puzzles!

THIS IS A BOX.

THIS IS A ROW.

THIS IS A SQUARE.

THIS IS A COLUMN.

Try to solve them all!

Here Comes Diego!

ANIMAL RESCUER!

CLUES

Feathered Friends

CLUES

6

Baby Jaguar

7

Water Action!

African Adventure!

GOOOAAALLL!

CLUES

Penguin Pals

Stay on Track!

MY TREE FROG FRIEND!

Swim! ¡Nada!

A Blast from the Past!

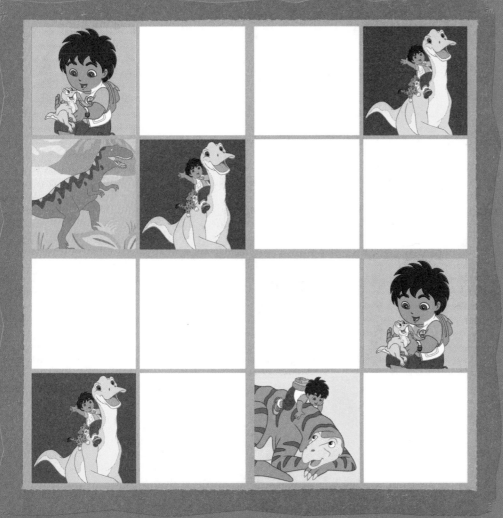

Sammy the Sloth

CLUES

16

Animal Rescue Center

 # ¡La Familia!

CLUES

Untamed Slopes!

CLUES

I'VE GOT YOUR BACK!

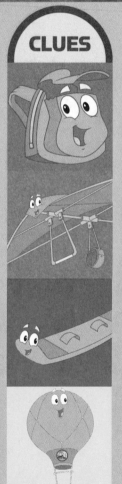

Up the Mountain!

Furry Friends

BEACH BUDDIES!

23

Monkey Business

Down the Rapids!

CLUES

The Bobo Brothers

CLUES

What a Team!

Let's Play!

Answer Key

P. 4 Here Comes Diego!

P. 5 Animal Rescuer!

P. 6 Feathered Friends

P. 7 Baby Jaguar

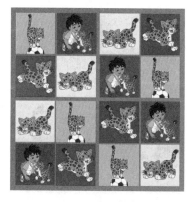

P. 8 Water Action!

P. 9 African Adventure!

P. 10 Goooaaalll!

P. 11 Penguin Pals

P. 12 Stay on Track!

Answer Key

P. 13 My Tree Frog Friend!

P. 14 Swim! ¡Nada!

P. 15 A Blast from the Past!

P. 16 Sammy the Sloth

P. 17 Animal Rescue Center

P. 18 ¡La Familia!

P. 19 Untamed Slopes!

P. 20 I've Got Your Back!

P. 21 Up the Mountain!

Answer Key

P. 22 Furry Friends

P. 23 Beach Buddies!

P. 24 Monkey Business

P. 25 Down the Rapids!

P. 26 The Bobo Brothers

P. 27 What a Team!

P. 28 Let's Play!

31

¡Felicitaciones!
Congratulations
on solving
all those puzzles!

You're not only
a great Animal
Rescuer—you're a
SUDOKU SUPERSTAR!

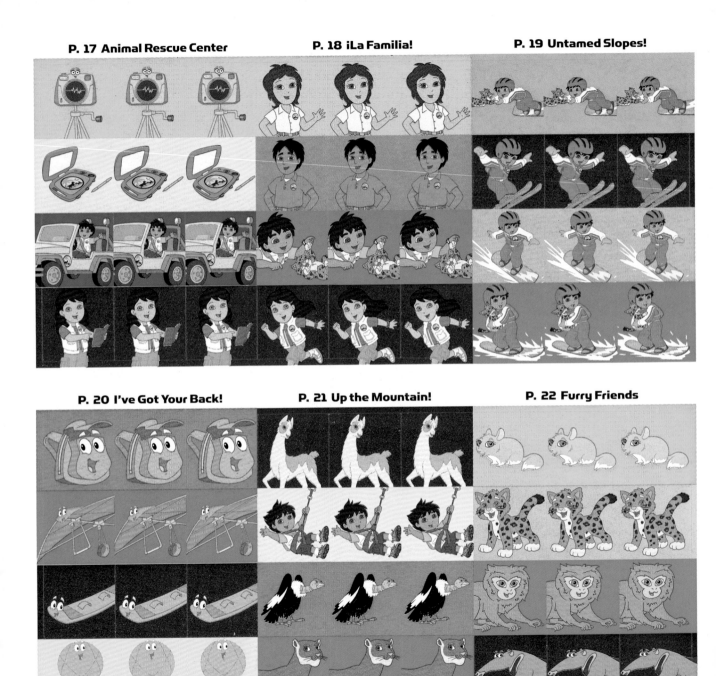

P. 23 Beach Buddies!

P. 24 Monkey Business

P. 25 Down the Rapids!

P. 26 The Bobo Brothers

P. 27 What a Team!

P. 28 Let's Play!